Also by Andersen Prunty

Sunruined: Horror Stories
The Driver's Guide to Hitting Pedestrians
Hi I'm a Social Disease: Horror Stories
Fuckness
The Sorrow King
Slag Attack
My Fake War
Morning is Dead
The Beard
Zerostrata
Jack and Mr. Grin
The Overwhelming Urge

PRAY YOU DIE ALONE

ANDERSEN PRUNTY

GRINDHOUSE PRESS

Published by Grindhouse Press
POB 292644
Dayton, OH 45429
www.grindhousepress.com

Pray You Die Alone: Horror Stories
Grindhouse Press #011
ISBN-13: 978-0-9849692-3-4
ISBN-10: 0984969233

Pray

You

Die

Alone

Contents

The Summer of Flies

In May, Marcus thought of it as the hottest summer he could remember. By August, he thought of it as the summer of flies. But it wasn't just the flies that were bad that summer. All of the other insects seemed to be out in abundance, as well. Every day, waking up in his fly-infested apartment, he would find another mosquito bite, looking more like a welt. The flies were the gross kind, slow and green, the kind Marcus always imagined liking shit. Another disgusting thing Marcus realized about the flies—where there were flies, there were maggots. He imagined them under the damp kitchen tile in his apartment, squirming together in trashcans throughout the town, preying with militant glee in the graveyard.

The maggots were there. The flies were there. But the flies, as they swarmed and irritated everyone, were not the only things making the summer memorable. There were also the disappearances.

The early afternoon temperature was in the mid-90s. It would hover around 98 before the sun went down in the evening.

Marcus had finished sweeping up those fat flies littering the floor, the victims of daily pesticide spraying, when he decided to go sit on his second-story apartment balcony and lazily flip through the classifieds.

Not finding any jobs, he put the paper down, lit up a cigarette, and leaned back.

Fuck it, he thought. I'll look tomorrow.

It was eleven o'clock and he already wanted a beer.

Marcus contemplated going to the refrigerator to get one when something caught the corner of his left eye. It was a girl, a teenager by the looks of her, wandering aimlessly down the sidewalk. Her bright orange tank top was what caught his eye. The thought of what was underneath held his gaze.

She also wore a pair of cut-offs and Marcus watched her legs as she sat down on the retaining wall in front of the library.

Probably waiting on someone, he thought.

He stood up, arched his back, and went into the house for that beer. In the kitchen, he took his time. He'd drunk ten of the twelve-pack last night, contemplated waiting until later and then convinced himself he would just drink the last two, since he'd have to leave to get more anyway. A big black roach, the size of his thumb, scurried under the refrigerator. Marcus watched it with bland indifference.

He went over to the turntable, flicked a couple dead flies off the dusty plastic lid, and put on a Ramones record, turning the speakers so he would be able to hear it from out on the porch. He didn't think the neighbors would mind. He hadn't seen them for days. Grabbing a fresh pack of cigarettes from the carton on top of the refrigerator, he went back out onto the balcony, ready to do some heavy duty lazing. He became nearly giddy with the prospect. This is what every American wishes he could do, Marcus thought.

The girl was still there, looking this way and that. Like she was waiting for someone. Marcus drank her in, wondering if she even noticed him up there. He got up to change the record three times. He'd smoked through half the fresh pack of cigarettes, finished up the second beer, and had to dip into the Johnnie Walker Black.

The girl never moved.

Christ, he thought, she has to be baking.

But that wasn't all he thought. What he really thought about was the complete oddness of the situation. Ever since May, there had been two to three disappearances a week which, in a town like Green Grove, significantly diminished the population. He knew many families, especially those with kids, had fled the Grove. The police force, small to begin with, was depleted. But fear became the new law, exercising its control. As he sat there staring at the girl on the wall, it dawned on him that she was the first person he'd seen outside in nearly a week. He hadn't seen any children or teenagers in probably a month.

After another shot of scotch and a joint, smoked with abandon on the small stoop, he decided it would simply be the neighborly thing to do to offer her a ride. Maybe she was in shock or suffering heat exhaustion or something. He pulled on a t-shirt and went downstairs, crossing the street in the midst of the lengthening shadows. Unlike a lot of girls in the Grove, this one got more attractive the closer he came to her. Her body filled out the top and shorts and Marcus put her age at sixteen or seventeen. And, at that point, his interests weren't solely prurient. She looked lonely. If, as he drew closer to her, he noticed a lazy eye and a harelip, he would have still offered her a ride.

"Get the fuck away," she spat at him just as he was ready to open his mouth.

"Look, I was just going to offer you a ride."

"I don't need one. Fuck off."

He thought about arguing but, as he opened his mouth, he realized he was way too hot, high, and drunk to go forward with it. Instead, he retreated slowly and cautiously back to his apartment where he shut himself up in the bedroom and turned the ancient window air conditioner up to its most frigid level. He made himself comfortable under the sheets and drifted off into some winter dreamland.

When he woke up, he put a Miles Davis record on and went over to the balcony to take in the evening air and smoke. He opened the door and nearly tripped over the girl sitting on the balcony. Surprise ran through her eyes as she adroitly leapt to her feet.

"Oh. I'm sorry. I didn't know it was *you*," she said.

"It's okay," he said. "I don't know what your problem with me is."

"It was shady up here. It looked cool, all right."

"That's fine. You could have come in if you knocked. I have an air conditioner."

"And I'll tell you what my problem is…" She wiped a sweaty strand of brown hair off her forehead. "My problem is these disappearances."

"I've heard about those."

"I'm sure you have. Anyway, I really need to find out who's doing this and I thought to myself: I'll just go stand someplace and mind my own business and the first person who comes along and offers to give me a ride or any shit like that, that has to be the murderer…"

"I don't quite understand your logic. So you think

murderers are basically friendly people? And besides, how do you know they were murdered? They could have just run away. Or been kidnapped or something. Or gotten sick and been part of some government cover-up. I've thought about these things too, you know."

"No, they were murdered." She looked at a spot somewhere off behind Marcus, phasing out, before snapping into the present and saying, "Hey, give me a cigarette."

"How old are you?"

"Look, burn out, I'm not a cop."

"Okay. You want some pot?"

"I'm not a burn out, either. Sorry."

Marcus flipped a cigarette through the torn opening and held the pack out to her, taking one for himself. He was afraid she was getting ready to go and realized he kind of wanted her to stay. It was somewhat intoxicating just to be standing close to her, smelling her scent. How long had it been since he'd talked to anyone except the old man at the carry-out?

"So," he said. "What makes you think these are murders?"

"I know where the bodies are."

Marcus coughed out a sputtering spume of smoke. "You what?"

"I've seen the bodies. I've counted them. The paper said there's only been ten disappearances, but there's been a lot more than that."

"Like how many?"

"Uncountable."

"You wanna come inside?"

"Bet you'd like that."

"I would. A lot, actually. You wanna come in and sit down?"

"You wanna go for a ride?" she said in a voice mockingly similar to his.

"Look," he said. "That's weird shit." But even as he stood there, rambling, thinking she was probably the crazy one, he knew he was going to say yes. He had to say yes because she was standing there in the damp night air, the nearly-full moon illuminated just over top and to the left of her head, casting an exotic purplish glow over her face. And there was this look in her eyes. Something that made her seem either incapable of lying or so hypnotic that a small lie, even a huge one, didn't really matter.

"I'll be waiting down on the sidewalk," she said.

He looked at the back of her neck. She had her hair pulled up and he noticed she had a small mole to the left of her spine and just under her hairline. Marcus went inside and grabbed the keys.

When he got down to the street, she was standing beside his truck.

"It's unlocked," he said.

"I'll drive."

"Do you have your license?"

"No. Does it matter?"

He tried not to look at her. It was when he looked at her that his will power seemed to break. She brushed a fly off her chest. Marcus tossed her the keys.

"Are you even sixteen?"

"You seem to have this hangup about age."

"I have a hangup about being arrested."

"Just relax. I've been wandering around all week and haven't seen a single copper."

"Where are these bodies?"

"Do you know where Womack is?"

"Womack's a long road. Which part of Womack?"

"Out near County Line."

"Okay."

She seemed way too small for the big truck. He enjoyed looking over at her seat, watching her leg muscles as she worked the accelerator and clutch. She'd obviously driven before. They slid along all the back country roads, in between the deep, high fields of corn, never passing another vehicle. Reaching Womack, they turned left.

Womack was an amazingly straight road. That was the thing Marcus had always found interesting about this part of Ohio. One minute, you might find yourself on a road with so many twists and turns, ups and downs that it felt like Tennessee. The next minute it would be flat and straight as Kansas.

"So, you've seen these bodies, huh?" Marcus asked.

"Yes," she said.

"By the way, what's your name?"

"Does it matter?"

"Yeah. Kind of. Unless you want to be remembered as 'That Girl.'"

"Maybe I don't want to be remembered at all."

"God, you're difficult."

"My name's Ellen, okay. Relax."

She had the truck up to eighty, the old tires flapping away under the rusted body.

"So do you really think going back to look is going to solve anything?"

"Maybe."

"What are you hoping to find?"

"The killer, for one thing."

"So, you're hoping he comes back?"

"So far, he's come back again and again. At first I find two dead bodies. Then there are four. Then eight. And now…"

"Think maybe you should have told the police?"

"I told them after the first two."

"And they're still there?"

"Go figure."

"I think you're fucking with me."

"I don't see much point in that."

"Maybe you're just taking me out here so you can kill me. Do you have a gun?"

He reached over and put his hand on the back of her shorts, knowing there wasn't a gun there. If there had been one, the shorts were way too small to hide it. She swerved the truck savagely to her right, dredging up the dirt shoulder and rolling him back to his side.

"Get the fuck off me!" she shouted. "How do I know that you didn't come along just so you could get me out here and rape me."

"More and more, it's starting to cross my mind."

"That's not even funny."

"Fuck you."

"Don't you even care that people are dying?"

"Of course I care, but you have to understand how abstract this all sounds to me. You just seem crazy."

"Shut up."

"I mean, come on, you sit outside all day when it's like a hundred fucking degrees. I try to give you a ride and you tell me to get the hell away. Then I find you curled up on my porch and begging for a ride. After accusing me, in so many words, of being a murderer."

"I told you… it looked shady up there. And I don't beg for anything."

"Let's just go see the bodies. My name's Marcus, by the

way."

"Oh."

"Oh?"

"I don't care much for the name Marcus, is that okay?"

"Whatever."

Ellen slowed the truck way down and came to a stop by the side of the road. She creaked the door open and hopped out. Marcus got out his side and walked around the front of the truck.

"I don't see any bodies," he said.

"The bodies are way back there." She pointed to a narrow dirt path, perhaps big enough for a tractor. If he had driven down the road with the corn this high, he wouldn't have even noticed it. "You have to walk back this little path quite a ways. Just before the corn becomes the woods, there's like this clearing… that's where they are."

"Couldn't we have done this during the day? Why does he just leave them out in the open?"

"It's not exactly out in the open back there, is it? Besides, most of those serial killer types want to get caught."

"You bring a flashlight?"

"Did you find a flashlight when you felt me up back there? It's a full moon. What more do you want? Look, it's bright enough to see your shadow."

It *was* amazingly bright. Ellen headed for the path and Marcus went behind her, watching the moon light up her body and trying to figure out how many months it had been since his last sexual encounter. He realized that, by focusing on the prospect of sex, he relieved a little bit of the uneasy tension twisting his neck muscles up in knots.

"Why didn't we just drive back here?" he asked her.

"I didn't want to surprise anyone."

"How long is it?"

"Probably almost a mile."

"How did you find this place, anyway?"

She didn't answer immediately. He almost asked her again, thinking maybe the crispy rustle of the corn and the crickets had drowned him out, but then she said: "Me and my boyfriend used to come back here."

"Oh, all that personality and she puts out too."

"It was more than that. We were gonna get married when we turned eighteen. This place was kind of like what we thought marriage would be like. You know, kind of a place away from the parents."

"A secret place."

"Yeah. Or so we thought."

"What happened to your boyfriend?"

"He was the first to go. The first to disappear."

"I'm sorry."

"We should be quiet now."

They continued down the moonlit path, in silence, for a few minutes. The clearing was now in eyesight. It was like driving toward the ocean and finally coming upon that strip of blue beneath the horizon.

"Follow me," Ellen said, cutting to her left and into the corn. At the perimeter, she turned and barked, "Quickly."

Marcus was suddenly and overwhelmingly filled with terror. Maybe it was just the fog of his various addictions, but he hadn't really taken any of this seriously until now. All the childish fears, those moments when certain feelings washed over him and lit that burning pit of dread in his stomach, all came scouring over him, rooting him to that narrow dirt path. He looked over to where Ellen entered the corn and the absence of her by his side forced him to move.

The corn was sharp and itchy on his arms. A hand reached out and took his.

"Come on," Ellen pulled him after her.

Blindly, they made their way through the corn, still headed toward the clearing but comforted with a blanket of seclusion.

"Why don't we just run for the truck?" Marcus thought about his sunny, music-filled apartment and realized he desperately wanted to be back in it.

Ellen turned around, getting closer to him than she had been all evening. Her eyes were wild, dancing around in her head, an indiscernible color. "I'm not turning around now. I have a lot more in this than you. If you're scared then just stand here. That'll be safer than running back to your truck. But I'm going some place where I can see that bastard throw out another victim. I'm gonna get close enough to see his face."

Marcus lowered his head. He didn't have a macho streak in his body but she had somehow made him feel low. He began to understand the significance this had for Ellen.

"I'll come," he mumbled.

"Then let's go," she said.

There was enough of a breeze so their movements weren't too noticeably loud. Nevertheless, the closer they felt they were getting, the more they slowed down and tried to squeeze between the stalks. Once they could see the clearing, they stayed back in the corn, using it like a security blanket.

In the distance, Marcus saw the bodies.

There was something infinitely sad about the way they were piled up there in the clearing.

Knowing the answer, he turned to Ellen and whispered, "Is that… them?"

Gravely, she nodded her head and said, "Let's move in a little closer."

"What about the killer?"

"I don't see him."

Well, that's obvious, Marcus thought.

Stepping out of the corn was like losing your clothing. They were naked now. If there was a killer on the loose, running around stark raving mad, they had little chance of hiding now. Running, maybe, but hiding was definitely out.

Marcus followed Ellen.

The grass in the clearing was worn down, as though it had been trampled quite a bit. Marcus thought it was probably from someone driving a truck out here. As they drew closer to the body pile, the stink intensified to a truly nauseating level. Marcus grabbed Ellen's arm. She turned to look at him, her stare pinning him where he was. Since coming out here, something had changed about her. She came off as a little flaky before but now she just looked insane.

"I don't think I can get any closer." Marcus pulled his shirt up over the lower half of his face.

"Have some fucking respect, Marco," Ellen said, shaking his grip from her arm.

Through the noisy, insectoid country night, Marcus heard a singular sound resonate—the humming of flies. *My God, there must be millions of them on those bodies.* He even thought he could hear the wet squirm of the maggots twisting through decomposing flesh. His gorge rose and sat stinging at the back of his throat.

"I'm gonna go wait in the truck," he said.

Ellen turned to him once again. The craziness was gone. She had put on her seductive face. Pouty and girlish, it was the look she had used to get him to give up his keys. "Come on Marcus. It's just a few more steps. You'll get used to the smell."

"Why don't you tell me what we're really doing here and I'll think about staying."

"But you're already thinking about staying, aren't you. Don't you know what we're doing here? We're trying to find the killer, remember?"

"If that was the case then why aren't we still hiding out in the corn?"

"You can't catch anything by hiding."

"Nobody said anything about *catching* anything. I'm not a cop."

Marcus looked into the heap, arranged in a semi-circle. It had to be most of Green Grove in there. Exposed to the elements, they had decomposed rapidly, their skin gray, pieces of skin peeled back, probably the result of wild animals. All of them were rendered unrecognizable.

Ellen wandered right up next to the bodies and dropped down onto her knees.

"What the hell are you doing? Can we just go?"

"I'm saying a prayer. Can't I do that?"

"Just hurry the hell up."

Marcus turned around and looked up at the moon. What a night this was turning out to be. He turned back around and Ellen was back on her feet.

"Come here," she said.

"I'd really rather not."

"I'll make it worth your while."

"Jesus," he muttered, thinking, I'm here anyway, aren't I?

He slowly walked over to her and she turned, grabbing him around the waist, pressing herself against him. Her eyes gleamed with a wild urgency. He bent down to kiss her and leaned into the smell of a hundred rotting corpses. She fastened her mouth around his, trying to bring him down to the ground. His stomach fought to come up and he put his hands on her hips, nearly encircling her bare midriff, to try and push her away.

He felt the twitching of her skin like something was fighting to get out. Just when he couldn't hold the vomit anymore, he let go, but it was forced back into his throat. He coughed and backed away, stumbling to his knees. Before he could stand up, his stomach convulsed again and he heaved, expecting the wet acid of his puke. Instead he felt the flies crawling over his tongue and all around the inside of his mouth. He looked back at Ellen and the crumbling wall behind her. The corpses were animated, Ellen standing at their center, flies crawling through her hair, covering her eyes and body.

Marcus bolted toward the corn, but the dead were there also. They had shifted, surrounding him. Flies crawled from their skin and hollow eye sockets, forming a cloud that blotted out the moon's glow.

The circle tightened and Marcus waited to feel their hands on his body. From behind him, Marcus heard Ellen whisper, "You're the last one, Marcus." And he felt her hands, hands that he would have welcomed a half an hour ago, slide down his stomach and crush his sex in an unforgiving grip.

"What happens now?" he begged.

"You taste death," she whispered. "The killer is here, somewhere. Only he didn't kill just my boyfriend. He killed me too."

"What does this have to do with me?"

"A soul is not free until his work is done. He made that clear. You're the last one." With that, Ellen snapped his neck and let him fall to the ground.

The Summer of Flies

It was a strange night that Marcus spent, lying on the ground, his body getting colder, his heart inactive in his chest. By morning, he had joined the pile, become food for the flies as he remained still throughout the rotting day. The next night, the dead rose again, dragging with them their veil of flies, and moved in to the next town, each of them intent on doing what had been done to them, hungry for some shred of justice.

Deathtripping in New Orleans

For two years, Tod Hoskins had followed a voice.

The voice was an insubstantial, shadowy thing. He was never really sure if it was inside his head or coming from somewhere externally, brushing past his ear like a moist whisper. Sometimes, he didn't think it was a voice at all.

No, it *was* a voice and it *did* have an owner.

Unfortunately, Tod was only able to find this owner during moments when he doubted his mental faculties the most: just before sleep or immediately upon awakening, deep in the throes of drunkenness or simply in a darkened room where space was nonexistent and time yawned like an empty chasm.

Sometimes he thought he wanted the voice to go away. Sometimes he thought he could chase it away so the only voice left in his head would be his own. But he knew that wasn't true.

If he lost the voice, then he lost *her*.

Her.

The voice was the last thing he had to remember Althea Jones.

It was *her* voice that called to him, nearly inaudible, intangibly soft, teasingly close, impossibly distant.

The voices had started after the car crash, two years ago, when they were both seventeen.

Tod was the passenger. He lived, emerging from the accident without a scratch, merely suffering from shock. Althea had died instantly, the steering column pulverizing her chest, crushing her heart.

Now, only memories and her voice. He did what he thought the voice wanted him to do, going wherever it told him to go.

Now it was September and Tod found himself standing at the far end of Jackson Square in New Orleans at the edge of a hurricane and he couldn't think of any reason he was there, save for the voice.

He wasn't a stranger to the city. His family had lived there until he was twelve, before moving to Ohio. He had always liked New Orleans. It seemed to have more than just a physical presence. There was another layer, another dimension to it. Maybe it was the strange history of the city itself. Maybe it was the city's fascination with things like voodoo and the dead. All those rumors of vampires and zombies. Maybe it was the heat and the humidity. Undoubtedly, it was all of these things, forming a ghastly mélange that crouched in the brain and wrapped the skin.

He liked being there. Not only was he following the voice, he also took an adult view of at least one part of his childhood. Something that made him think about full circles and how beginnings are so often endings. Tonight, however, would be his last night.

He would leave feeling somehow empty and unfulfilled. He had become accustomed to disappointment. Many times, he had gone where Althea's voice told him to go only to find nothing there. And so far, there didn't seem to be anything here either. Just emptiness.

According to the weather reports, a hurricane was only a few hours away. People had begun fleeing the city this morning. Tonight, it was practically empty. Businesses, not all of them, but most, had closed up, the owners shuttering their windows and going someplace safe to pray that the winds didn't tear their buildings down.

He had always thought of any tourist city as being very similar to a whore. Visitors come to leave their money, have fun, and maybe look at the beauty, however decadent, she has to offer, but then they leave with only a foggy memory. And tomorrow, by plane or by bus, he would do the same.

For now, there was the gentle beauty of the nearly empty city, the damp darkness softlit by gas lights, and the winds that were hard, constant and vaguely refreshing coming, as they were, at the end of a massive heatwave. He continued walking through Jackson Square thinking he had never seen it without any pedestrians or musicians or tarot card readers. There was something spectral about the empty benches.

But Tod was wrong. The Square wasn't completely empty. Maybe it had just been the murkiness of the night, but he had failed to notice the man sitting at the far end of the walkway. The man sat on a red milk crate, a brown man in a brown suit strumming a battered brown acoustic guitar. Tod came up behind him, veering off to the man's left so he didn't startle him. Tod waited until he was parallel with the man and began circling back toward him. The musician noticed Tod and nodded an acknowledgement.

Tod couldn't tell if the man was playing a song or not. The man strummed the guitar and hummed a tune that was maddeningly familiar but still unnamed. A small white bucket sat in front of the musician and he nodded toward it. Tod always hated it when the street performers more or less asked for money. But something inside of Tod felt sorry for this poor guy, sitting on the edge of a hurricane and playing to an empty street. Tod reached into the pocket of his jeans, pulling out a dollar and approaching the musician.

Tod leaned down to put the dollar in the bucket before the musician's leathery hand reached out to block him.

"You hang onto your money," the man rasped.

"No, you deserve it," Tod said.

"I'm not asking for money." Tod looked at the man's watery green eyes. The man looked down, voicelessly telling Tod to look in the bucket.

When Tod looked into the bucket, he saw that it was filled with black and white flyers.

"Take one," the old man said. "That's your free admission to a bit of fun on this most lonesome of nights."

Tod picked one of the flyers up, read it, and said, "Thanks."

The man nodded. Didn't say anything.

Tod glanced down at the flyer in his hand.

"But there's no address," he said.

"You'll know it when you get there. It'll be the only place with its lights on."

The voice, Althea's voice, whispered across Tod's ear, sending a shiver down his spine. He knew he would go.

"Well, thanks again," he said to the musician before turning and walking away.

"Have fun," the man said and went back to strumming his guitar.

Tod looked down at the flyer in his hand. It was an index card-size piece of white paper and, in big black blocky letters, it said:

FREE
SHOW

Simple enough, he thought. Now I just need to find it.

He nodded to the guitar player and turned around. A brief moment of hesitation filled him and he considered turning back to the guitar player and asking, "No, really, where is it?" but decided not to. A man who followed voices of dead girls to strange cities across the United States could not really spend too much time questioning himself about where he should go. Instead, he held the flyer out in front of him, almost like a flashlight. He glanced up at the green and white-striped awning of Café du Monde, noting the umbrellas on the tables had been removed, and turned to his left. The guitar player was right. Except for the street lamps, there wasn't a single light glowing. No one was home. The city's emptiness grew ever more palpable.

Aimlessly, he wandered up a couple of blocks and turned left.

Aside from the darkness, the city was ominously quiet. The only thing he heard was the wind in his ears. With a sudden exhilaration, he wondered when the hurricane was going to break over the city.

Damage.

That was what all the news reports had predicted.

Severe damage.

And he decided he didn't care. If he was going to be caught out in the storm, he welcomed it. He wanted it to rage over him. He wanted the cold air to strip back his skin, lay his soul bare and run its icy fingers through him.

If it killed him, it didn't matter. Two years of misery had him convinced that any sort of happiness, any lifting of his

21

black cloud, was not going to come. Maybe that was why he heard the voice. Maybe that voice was death. Maybe that was what he secretly hoped for every time he boarded an airplane or got in his car and raced down the highway. Maybe he wanted some fiery death to claim him, twist his body up with metal.

And he knew Althea would hate him for thinking that.

Althea – the beautiful young girl with the old-sounding name. And just thinking her name sent a tight shiver down the center of his body. That feeling bothered him. There was almost as much fear as love in that feeling.

Lost in his thoughts, he stopped when he came to an opening in between buildings. An alley. Looking down the alley, he convinced himself he saw a light gleaming somewhere back there. On the building to his right was a black sign with white lettering advertising the opening as Ohio Alley. He had never heard of it. Normally, if the city wasn't deserted, he would not have wandered down a dark, narrow alley but surely the pickpockets and thieves wouldn't see a profit in stalking a dead city.

With the paper still held out in front of him, he started down the alley.

And that's when he first got the feeling that, somehow, things just were not right. The darkness, the emptiness, the quietness—all of that was explained away by the hurricane. That was not part of the strangeness he now felt.

Now, being in the alley, it felt wrong. The buildings were higher than he remembered them. And they weren't just darkened, they were black. The broken cobblestones beneath his feet didn't feel entirely stable. They felt spongy, threatening to open up and suck him down. This was a prospect he would have completely welcomed. He wanted the earth to take him. It was what happened in the end, eventually, inevitably, anyway. Why not let it consume him now?

The air whistled through the cramped alleyway. For a moment, he felt like the alley was breathing around him, the mushy ground vibrating with a steadiness reminiscent of a beating heart. At the end of the alley, he could see faint yellow light pouring out of a door or a window. That had to be the place.

He walked the remainder of the way on legs that did not feel entirely his own.

The soft light at the end of the alley flickered in and out. *Were the winds that heavy?* he wondered. Could the power already be threatening to go out? It was possible, he guessed. Maybe the storm had already landed somewhere and would be on top of the city in no time at all. If that was the case, he should have been glad he was moving indoors only... he wasn't. He could have stayed out in it. He could have let it take him and that wouldn't have bothered him at all.

He reached the light. Something about it invited him toward it. It was meager lighting, not even bright enough to strain his night-focused eyes. The light invited him inside. Suddenly the light seemed the answer to his loneliness and his darkened mood. Inside, maybe there were people. And, inside, there was definitely that damp old wood smell he would forever associate with the city. It was a smell he found comforting. It reminded him of his grandma's house.

He stood in the doorway and, at that moment, couldn't remember a time when he had stood anywhere else. Suddenly, he didn't remember where he had come from and had absolutely no idea of the black death he had been chasing for the past two years. He had no idea where he was going.

He had no idea that was where he wanted to go because he was standing there in front of some kind of shelter. That was what the light and the scents told him. That this place was there to protect him.

There *were* people inside. Six of them. Three couples.

Tod went in to join them, still clutching the flyer in his hand like he would need it for admission. When he saw the others seated in old wooden chairs he knew he no longer needed his flyer and there was a sudden sinking inside of him. There wasn't anything to do here. It was just someone's idea of a cruel prank. Some malicious soul probably paid the street performer off to sit there and hand these false promises out to the last of the storm's stragglers.

But, because he hadn't felt quite right all night, Tod decided to sit down and give his legs a rest.

The others were seated in an evenly spaced out fashion, as though afraid of anyone else overhearing their hushed conversations. There were sixteen chairs. Four rows of four, separated by a narrow aisle. Tod counted them because he had nothing else to do. One of the couples stared intently toward the front of the dingy yellow room. Another couple sat in the back row and snickered over their own private jokes. The other couple stood up. They had been sitting in the first row and passed Tod as they left.

"This is some kind of fucking joke," the guy said.

"Yeah, like what the *hell?*" the girl said.

When they got to the door, the guy announced, "You all might as well go home. Nobody's coming. They do this all the time."

There was an uncomfortable tension before the guy finally escorted his girl out into the night. Tod understood the tension. He felt sure the others now felt exactly like the guy who had just left but to stand up and leave now would be too much like following orders and people do not often want to look like sheep. At least not overtly.

So that left the five of them waiting in the room with the flickering lights and the warm smell. The couple in the front row continued to stare intently forward, unmoving and not talking. The couple in the very back row continued their conversation. They were like himself and Althea, Tod thought. They could have gone anywhere. They were just happy to be in each other's company. Even if they were in a room staring at nothing. That didn't matter because they *were* each other's entertainment.

And now Althea was dead and Tod didn't think he could ever feel that again. He would never again feel what that giggling couple in the back row felt. That warmth. That belonging. That since of togetherness. Of being a part of someone else's life.

After thinking that last thought, the power went out.

The girl in the front row screamed and then things got really weird.

The room went black. Much blacker than it should have. Tod stood up from his rickety wooden chair and, upon standing up, lost his balance and collapsed to the floor. Whoever had been in the room with him before was now gone. He waited for a crack of thunder, a flash of lightning, anything. But all he got was the constant howling growl of the wind.

He didn't know what was happening.

The room swirled around him. He no longer knew where the door was or where it had been. He didn't know which way was the front of the room.

And he didn't care. He was ready to lie down on the floor

and let the entire structure rain down on him. That was what he had wanted since the beginning anyway, wasn't it?

But that didn't happen. The room shook violently, still in that disorienting black. He felt the wind rage over his skin and it didn't feel like anything he would run or seek shelter from. He liked the way it felt. It was cold in the stifling New Orleans humidity. Even more than that, it filled him with something he hadn't felt in a long time.

He didn't think he wanted to die anymore.

Now all he wanted to do was lie there and feel the wind rage across his body. That would have been enough for him. And as quickly as he thought that thought, the wind stopped.

He realized he had closed his eyes, half-expecting some kind of grim final climax to it all. But that wasn't what happened. Instead there was a quiet calm.

He opened his eyes.

He was no longer in the room.

He was outside of a cemetery and he wasn't lying down anymore. He was standing up, right in front of the twisted wrought iron cemetery gates hanging slightly ajar. To the right of the gates, someone had written the phrase "THERE ARE GHOSTS IN THIS CITY" in black spraypaint. For a moment, he didn't know if the graffiti was talking about the city of New Orleans itself or this city of the dead in front of him.

He could still smell the storm in the air but it was no longer on him, if it had ever even come. Maybe it had passed. Tod didn't have any idea. Looking around him, he wasn't even sure he was still in New Orleans. It was like the cemetery occupied a sphere of existence all its own.

In his ear, Tod heard the whisper—Althea. Beautiful Althea breathing across the side of his head, beckoning for him to follow her.

Tod walked into the cemetery, the mausoleums towering around him, some of them fresh and clean and gleaming white beneath the moon, others in a state of complete disrepair, as though whatever had once been contained within could come crawling out at any moment. From the corner of his eye, he saw a movement and from somewhere within the back of his brain, he found a memory.

It was a violent memory.

It surged up behind his eyes, the flashing whiteness of his car cutting into the electrical utility pole.

But it wasn't his car, he told himself. It was Althea's car. She had been driving and she had died.

He shook the memory from his head. That wasn't the Althea he wanted to remember.

The Althea he wanted to remember was in front of him, sliding past a crumbling gray tomb.

"Althea," he said.

"Tod," she said back. "We need to talk."

"I know."

"It's not what you think it is."

Tod drew closer to the ghost (was it a ghost?) in front of him.

"I know what you're going to say. I need to get on with my life. I need to stop following you. I need to stop trying to die."

"That's not it at all."

"What then?"

"I want you to join me."

Another memory, cascading through his brain, caused him to take a step back from Althea even though she was pale and beautiful and standing right there in front of him, everything he remembered about her made crystalline and drawn into sharp focus.

Why was he stepping back?

"We could do it, Tod. Me and you could be together. Just like we used to be. All you have to do is not go back. If you never leave this cemetery, you can be with me forever."

"I loved you, Althea." But even as he spoke the words, he doubted the weight of them. Doubted the truth of them. Another memory stabbed at him and he dropped to one knee. This one was harsh and fuller than the rest. More than just a fragment.

In the memory, Tod was driving the car. He fought with the steering wheel to keep the car on the road but it was a battle he lost. And there was something else in the car with him but not some*one*. There was something else in the car with him, in his head, and there was a reason he had aimed his car at the lone pole to begin with.

"You know you want this, Tod."

"No," he said. He stood up, shaking the memories out of his head, swelling with the new memories flooding into it. The memories he had had before the car crash. The *real* memories.

"I don't want it."

"Why not?" she asked, her lips gone pouty.

"Because you never were."

"But here I am, Tod. How can you say that I never was?"

"You were the figment of a lonely boy's imagination and when I wanted you to go you wouldn't and so I had to destroy what created you…"

"Yourself. Oh, you've grown so clever in your manhood. But dreams don't go away that easily, Tod. I will be with you until you die."

"No, you won't."

After saying that, the storm broke over the city of the dead. He crawled into an open mausoleum, one not yet used, to escape the winds and Althea crawled in with him.

The chill of the winds was replaced with all the warmth of a fever. The sweating thing that never was lay beside him in this cramped quarter, trying to coax Tod in any way plausible. Trying to get him to acknowledge her in some way because the more he acknowledged her, the more he addressed her, even if it was to tell her she was just something he had dreamed up, the stronger she became. So he lay there, huddled up into himself, his eyes drawn tightly closed as her hands roamed over his body and her breath swept his ear and his scalp. Hands and breath, nothing more. Nothing more physical than that. Nothing more physical than what could have passed as wind. Nothing there, Tod had to continue telling himself, listening to the cold winds around him and feeling so very hot inside. Like he was going to erupt in fire. But that was exactly what he couldn't do. When he had dreamed her up, Althea could do anything. She could take him to whatever pleasure limit his mind wanted to go. She could do all of that, Tod now realized, because she *was* his mind. He quivered, feeling the cool stone push against his fevered back, as he felt Althea's hands move lower and lower, reaching between his legs, preparing to administer the final test. Tod knew what she wanted. He knew she wanted to find rigid stiffness there. Hardness to enclose her breath around and then, eventually, her sex. She wanted to drag him back up within her.

But what she found was nothing. Tod started to laugh. A crazy man in a tomb during a hurricane trying not to let himself be raped by his own mind. He laughed away the past, fits of coughing turning into a bout of vomiting but, sometime during the course of this fit, he felt something whoosh out of him. His head, if it was possible, felt *emptier*. After that, he relaxed, sprawling back, his puke warm against his back.

He didn't know how long he stayed like that, but eventually he found blackness. A blackness more comforting than he ever thought.

It felt like years before he opened his eyes again. In reality, it was probably little more than a day. But, in another way, he realized, it was years. He felt like he had regained the lost years after the crash. He felt like he had regained a certain amount of sanity. A sense of purpose and a sense of light filled the space he had emptied. He slid out of the mausoleum and into the wet dawn.

He walked out of the cemetery and thought about trying to board a plane or a bus back to Ohio but he suddenly found he was terrified to step foot on an airplane. Maybe, he figured, this was the place to begin his new life. With his wet clothes sticking to his skin, he turned to his left, wondering how he had made it so far out here, and began walking toward the dark and sinking city before him.

Durning

The highway thrummed beneath them.

"It's nice of you to give up your break just to come with me," Christina Johnson said from the passenger seat, her delicately pale hand reaching out, stroking his knee.

Adam Strafe squinted into the sunlight beading through the dirty windshield and said, "I'm not really giving up much."

"I'm sure you miss your family, though."

"Maybe. I don't know. My parents are pretty preoccupied with the younger ones and... well, Maine isn't really pleasant this time of year. Not very springlike."

"I can't wait until you meet Mom and Dad. They're gonna love you."

"I'm looking forward to it."

That wasn't really true. Adam didn't really care about meeting her parents. He had a couple of motives for spending his break with her but meeting her parents definitely wasn't at the top of the list. First and foremost, he was hoping to finally be able to sleep with her. He had the whole scenario worked out in his head. Mom and Dad Johnson would make him a bed on the downstairs couch and he would sneak up to her room after lights out. This, he reminded himself, would be her teenage high school room. There would probably be posters of rock stars on the walls and stuffed animals tucked away in the corners of the closet. And there, maybe, he would have her.

"I might just have to show you off to the whole town," she said, smiling that perfect smile, all those straight white teeth beneath the freckled cheeks and coffee brown eyes.

"Durning, Ohio," he said. "I can't wait to see if it's everything you've made it out to be."

"Oh, it is. It's the perfect town. Almost magical."

Looking at her, he almost believed such a town could exist. He had met her in an undergraduate philosophy class at Shartles University in Pennsylvania. He sat to her right. He could almost smell the apple pie clinging to her hair. He was reminded of the part in *Annie Hall* when Woody Allen's character first meets Annie Hall and thinks of her as, "Annie from Wisconsin." That was how Adam thought of Christina. Christina from Ohio. Durning, Ohio, more specifically. The perfect town. Where the mail always ran on time and the neighbors not only knew but *loved* one another. That was his other reason for coming with her. He couldn't imagine such a town. Where he came from—Salt Port, Maine—the winters were long and mean and the people were almost as harsh. Growing up, he remembered the sky as a desolate slate of gray.

"So what's the weather like in Durning?" he asked, making small talk, car talk, something to while away the time.

"It's usually pretty nice. Especially this time of year. Not too hot, not too cold."

"Probably raining though, huh?"

Durning

"It doesn't rain that much in Durning. It must have something to do with the way the land lays or something. You know, like in the Pacific Northwest?"

He was clueless. He shook his head.

"There's Seattle, right? And everybody knows how much it rains there. But just to the east of Seattle, it's practically a desert. That's because of the Cascade Mountains. At least, I think it's the Cascades. They hold back the clouds and that's why it rains so much to the west of them but hardly at all to the east."

Ah, Christina from Durning, Ohio. Adam didn't know if anyone else could be truly enthralled by such trivialities. He loved it. It was almost enough to make him love her but he didn't know if he was ready for that yet. He didn't know if *she* was ready for that yet. It didn't seem like she had enough of the world on her. Let her season, let her experience some things, ferment, and then he would see what kind of person she would become.

Continuing on I-70 West through the mountains and the Amish country of western Pennsylvania, they crossed into Ohio and Adam asked if they were close yet.

"About another hour or so," she said, staring wide-eyed out the window.

They continued to make small talk. Christina talked nearly nonstop about Durning. He had heard about some of the people before. But she had different stories for them.

And pictures. She said she had taken a roll of film and went through town snapping pictures so she could remember them all. Adam glanced from the pictures back to the road, Christina narrating each picture. There was her dad, Thomas, smiling into the camera. He was a milkman. Adam said he didn't know towns still had milkmen. There was her mother,

Angelica. She was, of course, a stay-at-home mom. There was Town Hall. There was Memorial Park, in the center of town, landscaped perfectly, a wide expanse of lawn covered by picnickers and boys playing catch and girls playing with hula hoops. There was the soda shop/drugstore. Another throwback. And Mr. Daniels, the proprietor, wore one of those paper soda jerk hats on his head. Adam wondered if he was the pharmacist, also. He didn't know if he would want drugs from a man wearing a paper hat. The photos revealed women who were matronly but not unattractive. The men were lean and hard-jawed but their eyes twinkled with kindness. Unreal. Adam wanted to be cynical about the whole thing but it all sounded pretty good. After he finished doing all the things he felt like a young man had to do, he could see himself settling down in a place like Durning.

"Low on gas," he said, noticing the gauge bobbing in and out of the cautionary orange block.

"You should probably stop at the next gas station. That'll probably be it until Durning."

A few minutes later, he pulled into a gas station. They both got out, arching their backs in the pleasant air. It was early April and there was just a hint of summer balm in the air. Adam went around to the tank, twisted off the cap, inserted the pump and started filling.

"I'm gonna go in and get some coffee. Want some?" she asked.

"Sure. Thanks."

He put the pump on automatic and watched her as she walked in.

She was perfect. He didn't really want to admit that. He thought maybe he was too young to say he had really discovered perfection but there she was, strolling through the parking lot with her confident head held high. The pump stopped itself and he started for the store to pay. Spying him through the window, she motioned him away. She was paying this time too even though it was her car and she had paid before they left. He was okay with that. He would pay on the way back.

He got back in the car and watched her come toward him. Toward *him*. He couldn't really believe how she had even taken an interest in him. Maybe over the summer, he could take her back to his home town and show her the backwoods shacks, the abandoned houses downtown, the junked cars littering the yards of the shoddy suburbs. He grimaced at the thought.

"Thanks," he said as she slid into the car, handing him his jumbo Styrofoam cup of coffee. He took a sip. Gas station coffee always tasted like it was made with pencil shavings but it had caffeine and the caffeine was what he needed to get him through this last jaunt.

The last half hour or so they sipped their coffee and talked about other things, mostly common professors or projects they were supposed to be working on over the break.

She directed him off the interstate and onto a state route and then through some winding backroads. Ohio had yet to become flat and some of the turns were pretty wicked. Then they turned onto a gravel road and rose up a steep hill that wanted to be a mountain. When they reached the top she told him to stop the car.

"Here?" he asked.

"Yeah, you can see the whole town from up here."

"Oh, cool," he said. He always liked those sorts of bird's-eye-views of towns.

He eased the car over to the side of the road and downed

the last of his coffee. He looked at her and she smiled and made him feel things he had never felt before.

The road dropped away on her side of the car and he crossed over to her.

"Isn't it beautiful?" she asked.

He looked out over the valley and saw nothing. Was he supposed to see something? The only thing he saw was the gravel of the road give way to the grassy hillside and descend into a grassy meadow. A small knot of fear began in his gut.

"What are we looking at?" he asked, putting his arm around her.

"Durning," she said.

He had never thought she was insane before that instant and it was so fleeting he almost wanted to laugh it off.

He did laugh. A low chuckle that got caught up in the back of his throat. He coughed and felt his head swim. His vision blurring, the whole green meadow swooned in front of him. His stomach kicked up. Damn the coffee, he thought. Cheap ass gas station coffee always made his stomach burn. And when was the last time he'd eaten?

"I'm not feeling so well," he said.

"Maybe you need to lie down," she said, beaming, moving in, kissing him on the cheek, running a hand softer than cornsilk down his forearm.

"Yeah," he choked out.

He didn't even remember making it back to the car.

"You've finally come to," Adam heard Christina's voice through a thick haze.

Yes. He had finally come to. He wondered what had happened to him. He opened his eyes, expecting to feel her cool and comforting hand on his forehead.

Durning

But he had trouble opening his eyes. He couldn't focus. Once he finally got them opened, it still didn't feel right. His vision was limited. He couldn't see anything to his left. He felt that eyelid opening and closing but there wasn't anything there.

What the hell? he thought.

He tried to raise his hand to touch his eye because he didn't know why he couldn't see anything out of it and he wondered what that ache was. That ache, so hollow, throbbing at the border of his brain.

And why couldn't he move his arms?

Something was wrong. He was now sure of that. He was either more than just sick or... or Christina had done something horrible to him.

With his one eye, he looked down at his lap.

He was seated in a wheelchair.

A wheelchair? he thought. Maybe he had been out a lot longer than he thought he had. Maybe he had gone into some sort of coma.

No. No, that couldn't be. Looking ahead of him, he saw the meadow he and Christina had looked down upon only the sunlight had disappeared and a little wind had picked up and it felt a lot colder now.

His hands were strapped to the armrests of the wheelchair. His heart skipped and thudded in his chest when he saw that his right hand didn't look right. Three fingers were missing. It wasn't until noting their absence that he felt the pain there too. A different kind of pain than the one in his eye but a very real pain nonetheless.

Where was Christina?

He turned to view the panorama before him. He spotted her to his right. She was bent down about four feet from his wheelchair, her back to him.

"If you're wondering about your eye, I took it out."

He wanted to laugh. It had to be a sick joke but he knew she wasn't joking. He could see that some of his fingers were missing, why should he think his eye was anything but gone?

"*What?*" he coughed out.

"You heard me. If you're wondering about your eye, I took it. We needed a theater."

She patted the ground with her small hands and stood up, dusting them off on her jeans.

"Did you *plant* my eye?" he asked.

"Of course. How else would I grow a theater?"

She came over behind the wheelchair, leaned down close to his ear and said, "This is going to be the best town yet. I'm sorry you never got to see Durning. Kenneth Durning was this absolutely beautiful boy I met in Idaho. He was beautiful but so naive. You wouldn't believe the things I wanted to do to him. I told him all about those things but he wasn't interested. You could practically smell the fucking apple pie on him. So I planted him somewhere in Missouri. That's where Durning really is. It's a beautiful place. Real fucking pure. Just like him.

"I wonder what kind of place Strafe will be. I give the theater two months before they start showing porn."

Christina pushed the wheelchair along. Adam jostled himself about, trying to topple the thing.

"Just let me go, Christina. Let me go!"

"You know I can't do that."

"Why? Just let me go. I need a hospital. I need a doctor."

"The town needs a concert hall. Where do you think we should put it?"

Hot pain. Slicing down close to his scalp. Screaming behind

his ear.

Christ! She just removed his ear.

"Christina! Christina!" he shouted.

She walked in front of the wheelchair, in front of him, now to the other side of him, and planted his ear in the grassy ground.

Adam could feel himself sliding into shock. He realized he was alternately screaming and sobbing but he couldn't do anything to stop that. He couldn't help it. His chest rose and fell rapidly. He was very aware of the blood covering his body.

"Christina, just let me go and I swear, I swear to God I'll do anything you want me to just please please please don't do this."

"You talk too much."

She grabbed some other instrument from behind his head. It was a long knife. She drew it back on each cheek, severing all of the muscles controlling his jaw.

She doesn't want me to bite her, Adam thought. Oh my God, she doesn't want me to bite her. And that meant she was going to do something even worse.

She reached into his mouth and grabbed his tongue. Adam tried his hardest to jerk it away but she clamped with her thumb and fingertips and it hurt. Amazing, he thought, with all the other pains in his body, the way his tongue was able to take center stage and hurt the most.

Sticking the knife back to his throat, she drew the blade along the back of his tongue and the only sound Adam could make was with his now ravaged vocal cords. She held the tongue up in front of him.

"I wonder what we'll do with this. A tongue can become many things. A church that spits lies. A coffeehouse of bad poetry. A townhall of bickering dissent. The rundown house of the finest whore in town."

Adam sat in the chair, his body rigid, his one eye bulging toward Christina as she held the tongue up appraisingly. She turned to plant it in the ground. Now he couldn't smell any trace of apple pie on her. The only thing he could smell with his last trembling breaths was the stink of death and he didn't know from which of them it came.

Air Cathedral

The room choked on blue dawn bitterness.

"Why don't you show me?" Arthur asked the bleeding heap, the mere puddle of a human, behind him. Arthur did not look at the priest when he asked him this question. He sat in the old wooden chair, a blood-stained Styrofoam cup of cold coffee in his right hand, a burning cigarette in his left, staring out of the partially open window in front of him.

The man on the floor behind him didn't say anything. Of course he didn't say anything. Arthur figured he was probably dead. Beyond dead, even. Mutilated. Arthur fought the urge to turn around and look at him. To study him as some people study paintings, sculptures, or the beauty of a chosen sex.

He wanted to look at the priest because he thought the priest could show him something. Arthur still wasn't sure what this something was, but he knew it was there. It had to be in one of his victims or else his work had all been fruitless.

How many had there been?

It was countless.

Only, it wasn't really countless at all. Eighty-six. That was a very exact count. Eighty-six priests going back twelve years.

Arthur didn't know why he had chosen priests.

No, that wasn't true either. He chose the priests because they were eager for someone to hear their confessions. And Arthur was that person. Before using the knife or the gun or, in this case, the drill, he listened to their confessions. Everyone had confessions, he was sure, but there was something about the priests' confessions that seemed weightier. Maybe it was because they, after hearing so many confessions themselves, knew how to tell a confession. Or maybe it was because their confessions were somehow entwined with all the confessions they had heard over the years, like the confessions they'd heard were some kind of bassy backbeat to their own.

Some of the priests' confessions were quite nasty. Some of them made what Arthur was doing look like the work of a saint. Others were beautiful. These were the ones Arthur had the most faith in. These were the ones that filled him with the most hope.

Ultimately, he guessed he had initially sought out his first priest because that was who he had first shared his confession with. It wasn't just a confession. It was a dream. It was a life's journey. It was something he knew he had to find. He wasn't sure if it was a place or just a something, some disembodied structure lodged in the reaches of his subconscious, but he knew it existed and that it was out there somewhere.

Come to think of it, it was hardly a confession at all. When he had told that first priest, it was more like a statement or a declaration. The priest had scoffed at him. Told him it was all metaphor. Tried to tell him he was on the path to righteousness and he needed to follow the footsteps of Christ.

But, well, Christ had never done *this*.

Now he sat on the third floor of an old abandoned warehouse, looking out over the city, where people were just filtering out of their apartments, getting into their cars and going off to work. This was a world he was not part of. There was a certainty to this thought. A certainty that could not be denied.

This was a time of reflection for Arthur. Reflecting was something he was not a stranger to. He sat there and wondered why he had chosen this particular priest. It wasn't just accessibility. No. It was something in the old man's eyes. They were the same blue Arthur had seen in the sockets of a hundred Irish Catholic priests but there was something else to this man. There was a certain twinkle, a certain knowledge. And the complete ease with which this priest (who would not give Arthur his name) died hinted at something greater. Perhaps this man contained the peace and serenity Arthur had sought for so long.

He sat his cup of coffee down on the splintered wood windowsill, tossing the burnt nub of his cigarette into its dregs. He stood up and knocked the chair over as he did so.

"You're the one," he said as he stalked over to the body of the priest. "You have to be."

The priest was a mess. Arthur's gorge threatened to kick up as he approached him, knelt down beside him.

Arthur reached into the wound running down the priest's torso, pulling it open with his hands, leaning down into the sick warmth of his body, the smell of early decay already there.

He swooned, his balance thrown off. He pitched forward and thrust his arm out, his hand hit the blood sticky wall and he hovered above the priest, drunk off the rush of scent rolling around in his head.

He stood up and walked back over to the window.

Time had jumped forward.

This was not unusual for Arthur. Strange gaps in memory. Time racing forward. No, not racing, *jumping*, like frames cut from a film. He was here, he was still here, but everything and everyone around him was suddenly five minutes or a half an hour ahead. He had to catch up with it, time, them. He felt dragged along, a slight nausea slithering in the back of his head as he stepped into the present.

Time jumped forward. It always did.

The city bustled now. Thronging with a thick presence seemingly borne out of its hard, manufactured surface, the city bustled. Car horns. Shouting. The whole sick and violent world thrown into motion for yet another day. He looked west out the window, over the buildings, toward the heart of the city and that was when he saw it.

This was the first time he had seen it in twelve years and this time, this time, it wasn't just some image from a dream. It was something in front of him. In the distance but still vast. Vast and real, as solid as it could ever be and very much *there*.

The air cathedral.

He didn't know of any other way to describe it. It was like all the cathedrals of his boyhood only this one was more immense and promising and looked like something Dalí would have painted. It wasn't simply a bricks and mortar cathedral floating in the sky. It looked like it was actually inscribed in the air. There and not there at the same time.

A feeling came over him that he couldn't describe. Seeing the cathedral was not enough. He had to be inside of it. He had to walk its crystalline halls and look down at the strange worlds it hovered over.

Arthur walked back over to the priest.

"How do I get there? I know you know. How do I get there?"

But the priest wasn't talking.

Arthur went back over to the window. He shoved the window all the way up, never looking away from the cathedral glittering in the air miles ahead of him. He thought about jumping from the window but couldn't put that much faith in anything like that. And if he was wrong, that would mean his quest was over. He also thought about running through the street, never taking his eyes off the cathedral, just running until it was right above him. But one did not run down crowded city streets while covered in blood and reeking of death.

So he sat on the ledge, only to be closer to the cathedral, feeling the cold wind swirl up from the cold street.

It was truly beautiful, how it hung there in the sky, looking more like a castle than a place of worship.

Then things got jumbled up inside of Arthur's head. He didn't know what happened but, suddenly, he desperately wanted to be off the narrow window ledge. He wanted to be back in the room, his feet planted firmly on the ground. But he couldn't seem to move and when he finally managed to turn his head around, the priest was there behind him, smothering him in that bloody scent.

This could not be happening, Arthur's mind shouted. This could not be happening. Arthur faced the priest, noting the way the air cathedral gleamed in the reflection of each eye.

"You wanted me to show you," the priest spoke through vocal cords Arthur had ruined hours ago. "You wanted me to show you and I did."

Arthur wanted to speak. He wanted to argue with the man

but a loud bleating was the only thing that came out.

"And now you want me to take you there."

The priest pulled Arthur back into the room. The room was now full of people, all dressed similarly to the priest. Arthur didn't have to count them to know how many of them he would find. There were eighty-six of them in there and something screamed inside Arthur's head. These people were not priests. They were not priests at all.

"We can take you there," the priest said. "It is not a pretty place."

Suddenly, Arthur didn't want to go. He didn't know what he had been doing all these years. It fell away. His whole journey fell away or, rather, he realized that maybe it wasn't *his* journey but *their* journey. He felt all of their cold hands on him, looked at the wounds he had inflicted, and tried his best not to scream as they took him to the air cathedral. His life sprawled out behind him like a horrific photo album and all of that was nothing compared to what he was about to see.

The Nowhere Room

Anna Seifert sat in front of her computer, trying to work on a literary paper about the writings of Ambrose Bierce. So far, she hadn't made it any further than the title page. The cursor blinked in and out of the grayish-white background, after the terminal "t" of her last name.

It was a beautiful early summer day. She stared out the window. Her study felt like a prison. The window afforded a perfect view of the children across the street. Three kids who looked to be around the age of five ran around the neighborhood yard in an insane pattern, no doubt driven by a perfectly understandable kid-logic. The next minute, she was yanked from their sunny imaginings and thrown to the floor.

It had been a while since she'd had one of these attacks but she immediately recognized it for what it was.

Once again, her memory was trying to kill her.

On the floor, struggling to crawl across the carpet and pull herself up on something, her vision turned a screaming red.

Her head throbbed.

Her muscles knotted up.

Her gorge rose and she exploded a pool of stinking vomit, some unseen hand forcing her down into it.

And then she heard the voice, calling her name like metallic fire and brimstone scraping at the inside of her skull, the backs of her eyes.

"Anna!"

She tried to answer it, but her gorge came up again, turning her vocal cords acid and watery.

"Anna! Anna! Anna! Anna! Anna!"

The voice always liked to wait until she was alone. Sure, it removed embarrassment but it also removed any sense of comfort she might gain from those around her.

The angry swarm in her mind and viscera, like a vicious hybrid of psychic bees, screamed on for a few more minutes before leaving her stunned, squirming in her own vomit, piss, and shit. Her pride was gone someplace else but the past, the past was right there in front of her.

Anna saw a small abandoned house in a stand of trees behind an empty field.

She saw a small fire burning in a thickly rusted grill without legs.

She saw a sixteen-year-old girl named Carmen.

She saw visions and colors, some of them beautiful, some of them horrible. She felt a glittering, revelatory magic in her veins and felt it turn ugly.

She rose from her expulsion, went into the lonely bathroom and washed the stink from herself. It had taken years but she now knew what she had to do.

Once she started for Gibraltar, there was no turning back. Something pulled and pushed her along, forced the whining engine of her car to give as much as it could. Intent tunnelvision melted Anna's eyes to the road, keeping her mind free from distraction. Almost eagerly, she cruised along the boondocks, those rural islands of Ohio, sandwiched in between the industrial sprawls.

Soon, with the gray coming of dusk, she reached the tiny town of Gibraltar. It was roughly the same size as Red Oak, the college town where she taught, but completely different. It was precisely the beaten down, worker-drone mentality of Gibraltar that had pushed Anna through the ranks of the university. When she finally received her Ph.D. from a small school in Pennsylvania, she hung the certificate by her desk and it was only then she felt separated from Gibraltar. Wherever she moved afterwards, the doctorate came with her, hung someplace where she could see it nearly any time she wanted to—hung up as a reminder. She couldn't explain it, exactly. She just always had this fear that, without as much education as she could possibly get, she was forever in danger of sliding down some dark rabbit hole and becoming one of Them.

And now, as she entered the town, the same force that had been speeding her along slowed her down as if to say, "Look." She cruised down Main Street, her eyes scouring the shabby buildings, the run down storefronts, the three bars with spraypainted, particle-board windows. A man stepped out from one of the bars, his skin as gray as his hair, thin shoulders protruding from his ancient flannel shirt. He stared at the sidewalk as he ambled along, his whole body leaning toward the ground, toward some premature death. Anna thought they should change the town's name to Sorrow. The depressing sadness that had ridden with her the first eighteen years of her life was back.

Luckily, the town proper wasn't that large and she was soon

out on the state route, cutting through fields of low corn.

Memories trickled through her head and, for the first time in a long time, she thought of the Infinity Room.

Anna had discovered it the summer she was twelve and had immediately told Carmen about it. Carmen had dubbed it the Infinity Room without any real reason, they just decided they liked the name. Furthermore, it was a name they could agree on. The small, one room house in the middle of the woods became like a slice of adulthood for them. They went there and talked about whatever they wanted to as loudly as they wanted to. Sometimes Carmen stole cigarettes from her mother and, together, they smoked them in the Infinity Room. They got drunk their first time in the Infinity Room. Anna lost her virginity there when she was fourteen. It was with one of Carmen's cousins who had come down for the week. He was seventeen and told her he had already initiated Carmen. It lasted only a couple of minutes and ended with the boy awkwardly masturbating in her face. She didn't learn until later that was how they did it in pornos.

She cared nothing for the boy and nothing for the experience although, over the next couple of years, she took a few more boys to the Infinity Room. When she was sixteen, she realized she only liked boys as friends. Carmen was who Anna was attracted to. Other women would come later but, at the time, she thought only of Carmen. That summer, the Infinity Room blossomed into something very much like a house with Carmen and Anna playing the parts of newlyweds. Slowly, as the summer drew on and rotted into fall, a taint came over the Infinity Room. For the first time, there were arguments. The girls said things to each other they didn't really mean. Things were done that shouldn't be done. The winter and early spring were unbearable, a screaming black

The Nowhere Room

Rorschach blot of heartbroken teenage depression. It was here Anna's memory broke up and turned to static.

"Carmen," Anna said, barely audible. It felt good. It was a name that started all the way at the back of the throat, brought the lips together and exited the mouth with a soft air, the tongue left to caress the roof of the mouth.

"Carmen."

Her car left by the dirt access road, Anna approached the small house in the early moonlight, her heart leaping around in her chest. Choked with memories, she pulled open the door and stepped into the familiar smell of old rotting wood and all the familiarity of the past.

With an electric rush, it came over her. Veins pounding, skin crawling, she remembered what had happened on that April day just after turning seventeen.

It had been a rough morning. Anna had fought with Carmen the previous night and it looked like they might finally go their separate ways. Wanting to get away from her mother's questioning (*Are you using* drugs, *Anna? No boy's worth all this, Anna.*), she went to the Infinity Room.

She remembered everything now with a distilled clarity.

The way she had stalked up to the old house, wanting only to sit and sulk in one of its cool corners. Sit and sulk and be alone and think about how she would have to get used to that word: "alone." She remembered the way she had yanked the rickety old door back on its tenuously moored hinges. The way she had felt when she saw the boy on top of Carmen, working away. The look in Carmen's eyes that said, with glistening surprise, things could never be the same again.

Anna felt hackles rise all over her body. A previously unfelt electricity started in her stomach when she saw Carmen's hips, pale and perfect, below her upraised cotton dress, rising to meet the boy's thrusts. Unbridled, Anna felt the electricity, the energy, explode from her skin.

She screamed. Powerful and focused, she directed that energy to the sick revenge taking place on the floor of the Infinity Room. Then it was their turn to scream.

The poor boy didn't even know what hit him.

He had come down somewhere on the state route. The trucker who rolled over him said he never even saw him. It was like he came out of nowhere. The papers, of course, never said he fell from the sky. It was speculated the he had simply wandered out onto the road at the wrong time. There was alcohol in his system, never mind that it wasn't enough to write his accident off as a drunken mishap. The papers never mentioned Carmen and Anna. The girls were the only ones who knew about that, about Anna's awful power.

Carmen, poor Carmen, would never be the same again.

And Anna turned her back on it all. Left to throw herself into her studies, to busy herself with the creation of a purely intellectual world she could shape and control with all the tools of her trade.

Now Anna stood in the Infinity Room, so much cooler than outside. Outside where there was life—the rattle of cicadas, the chirp of crickets, the ever growing and twisting of the trees and vines. In here there were only memories.

Anna circled the small iron top of the thickly rusted legless grill, something she and Carmen had dragged here to build fires in. Fires that melted away their inhibitions and their childhood.

Looking down into it, she saw red-hot coals flicker and

ignite into a small flame.

Anna wasn't very shocked. She expected things like this to happen when she came back to the Infinity Room.

Looking around, she noticed not much had changed. There were new things spraypainted and chalked on the walls: OZZY RULES, THE BREW CREW, SENIORS 91, FUCK ME MARYLOU, POOPTOOTH LIVES. All of the scribblings stood out as epithets toward her memories.

Then she saw Carmen, faintly at first and then drawn into sharp focus. The insubstantial figure walked toward the fire, toward Anna, coming out of nowhere.

"Carmen," Anna said.

"Anna," Carmen said back.

"It's good to see you."

"You knew I would be here. I've always been here."

"Well, I knew you would be here in spirit."

"No, you saw to it a long time ago that I would always be here. Why did we call it the Infinity Room? Do you remember?"

Anna shook her head.

"We should have called it the Nowhere Room," Carmen said. "Because that's what it is. You know, I've been right here ever since that day, waiting for you to come back. I knew you would."

"You haven't been here since that day. I watched you walk away…"

"But I was never the same, Anna."

Anna used to like to hear Carmen say her name, but now it contained all the beauty of a racial slur. It was something spit or thrown out of the mouth.

Carmen continued, "You stole something vital from me that day. Just like how you managed to throw Peter nearly a mile away. You stole something from him, too. And you, you were too self-involved to even realize what had happened. What would your students… what would your precious *colleagues* think if they knew you could wipe them out with a single thought?"

"Carmen… I didn't mean… I was just so mad. I had no control over it. I never… It's never happened since. I've learned." Anna's body was trembling.

"The Nowhere Room, Anna. This is where you left my insides when you scraped them out. But you wouldn't know. You've never come back to visit."

Warm tears coursed down Anna's cool cheeks. "I'm sorry, Carmen… If I had known, I would have…"

"Would have what? Come back so you could piss on my soul. Take it out of nowhere and put it someplace worse. You say you had no control over it, but what about after that incident? What about when you saw me walking down the halls at school, a hollow shell? What about after I got sick and laid in bed for months? I had *strangers* coming to visit me, Anna. People I didn't even know. And where were you? Where were you at my funeral? Another room filled with strangers."

"My parents wouldn't let me go."

"You were nowhere."

Sobs and sadness rippled the muscles in Anna's face. She drew in a snotty breath and said, "Carmen, I only wanted to be with you… Since then, you're the only one I've thought about."

"Is that what it was all about? Because you couldn't have me. Because I liked boys better than you?"

"No," Anna sobbed.

"Well, you had me and then you let me go. I think you

could have brought me back from nowhere and I still think you will. I've learned some tricks of my own over the years."

"To say the least." Anna thought about the unseen forces that had attacked her over the years, things she had always thought were part of her own mind until earlier today.

"You've noticed," Carmen said.

Now Anna's black memories turned to an even blacker tumor of fear. From inside her head, she felt a sickening twisting metal feel, the one that had driven her to the floor earlier. But this time it pulled her toward the fire. The nausea blossomed like a mushroom cloud and she bent to throw up and found herself unable to fall to her knees, her puke hanging from her chin and sizzling onto the fire, fueling it rather than dampening it. And then she stepped into the small grill, felt the flames at her feet, licking at her jeans and crawling slowly upward until they licked at the backs of her arms, up her stomach, her breasts, her neck, her spine, her hair, her chin, her lips, her cheeks, her eyes.

And she heard Carmen's voice saying, "I'm going to get out of nowhere and you're going to take me. I am the fire around you. I am the Nowhere Room. I am the trees and the snakes and the wolves and the dirt and the air and the stars and the moon. I consume you, Anna. *I consume you.*"

Anna felt the fire burning the moisture out of her skin, shrinking it. She felt her skin crack and pop open and heard her vital fluids hissing onto the flames.

Slowly, skinless, Anna stepped out of the fire. With a new vision, she looked around the Nowhere Room and saw it for what it was: Nowhere. On tender feet, she crossed the warped wooden floor and exited through the door.

Outside, the balmy night breeze rustled the trees and moved over her moist, raw body. Everything was bright and purple and she felt magic snake through her exposed muscles and veins. Relishing the night, she walked deeper into the woods until she reached a small clearing. Here she smelled the earth's dark loam and almost thought she could smell each mineral in the soil, hear them slowly dissolve into the trapped rainwater. She felt the dark decay of the dead leaves and felt the slow growth, so full of life, of the trees around her.

Then she heard the banshee-like yattering of wolves, all of them responding to one another, their collective howls and yelps rising to an ear shattering crescendo.

They surrounded her.

"I am all that surrounds you," she heard Carmen whisper in her head.

Slowly, they closed their circle on her. These were not the beautiful, powerful wolves she recognized from nature photos. No. These were the Gibraltar version. What wolves looked like in Nowhere. They were thin and mangy, yellow-eyed and decrepit. Wild dogs. They looked so underfed they would eat anything and, eagerly, they sniffed at the meal at hand.

Anna was not afraid.

Fear was not an option.

She felt their wet muzzles on her glistening body. She felt their tongues lapping at her blood, sucking it from between muscle and tendon. Sensing the competition amongst them, they all tore in at once and Anna felt their broken teeth rip into her meat and drag her down into their pack. She felt and smelled their greasy fur rubbing up against her and longed for their filthiness. She felt one of them between her legs, nuzzling at her burnt sex before digging in with its teeth. She felt her meat come off her bones and stared up at that faceless purple sky, glittering with the icily indifferent stars. She felt herself go out into that sky, something inside of her rising above the wolves. She felt herself circling the earth, pulled toward the sun and burning up in the atmosphere, fires exploding behind her eyes and through her viscera and she exploding with them.

When she came to she was curled up beside a long dead fire in the thickly rusted legless grill of the Nowhere Room. The oily, burnt charcoal smell cloyed at her. Dawn trickled in through the windows.

She took deep breaths. She ran her hands down her body.

She was alive.

She was whole.

Thank God.

Slowly, like somebody coming upon a new world, she walked out of the woods and down the dirt access road walled in by those fields of corn.

She remembered leaving the keys in her car, ready to make a quick escape, and hoped no one had stolen it.

Heavily, she trudged along in the dirt until she reached her car, the door handle feeling cool, clean, and good.

Anna sat down and turned the ignition.

She reached for the power button on the radio, wanting some loud music to wipe away the darkness of the previous night. She still wasn't sure what had happened. Wasn't sure she really *wanted* to know.

With her fingers on the tuner, another voice, a foreign one, came into her head, "What are we going to listen to, Anna?"

"Carmen," she whispered.

Without controlling them, her fingers pressed the tuner until it landed on a jangly rock song.

"There, that's good," Carmen said.

Anna pulled away from the gravel roadside feeling both extremely sad and happy. She realized she no longer controlled her body, it was Carmen. From within her own head, she could feel out Carmen's thoughts and they were not her own. Carmen wanted to see her new house. Carmen wanted to meet her new coworkers, people who had only been faces across a metaphysical void. Carmen wanted to feel a man between her legs, his cock battering her insides. Nausea racked Anna but she had no way of being sick, her body no longer hers. Anna sensed the new duality of her existence, heard the yammering voice of another person's thoughts, and felt the first powerless fingers of madness.

"Welcome to the Nowhere Room." Carmen laughed with Anna's mouth, checked her soul behind Anna's eyes in the rearview mirror, and sped down the state route.

Black Rosita's Man

The hills were dark and the hills were mean. But, the rumor went, give Alistair Doos a guitar and things would lighten up a little bit. Judging by the crowd that turned out at the Downtrod Inn, he could make things lighten up a whole lot.

It was the crowd there on that Saturday night that amazed Nathan East. The music was expectedly astounding, but he had heard most of that from recordings. All the recordings took place in this same location—the Downtrod Inn, Sawmill, Ohio. Nathan looked at the crowd around him. He had hoped to be pressed against the stage but even halfway back in this tiny bar was a great place to be. People were packed in from the stage back to the actual bar and, beyond that, out the front door. If anybody wanted to sit and drink they had to do it out on the porch.

Looking around, it was easy for Nathan to divide the locals from the people like him—country blues fans whose curiosity finally got the best of them. It surprised him how many of the people there were white and how many of them looked like they should be listening to something a little more hip. When you're great, Nathan thought, it doesn't matter what type of music you play, your audience is diverse, to say the least. It was true, Alistair Doos wasn't one of the first blues musicians. At something like 70 he was too young for that, but he was certainly one of the best, if not *the* best. Nathan skeptically told himself that probably wasn't true. He wondered how many great musicians went unrecorded or, in a more hateful time, were completely excluded from the music world.

The main thing Nathan thought about was that he was here now. He had braved the state routes and the back country roads, gravel or dirt in many cases, to come and stand here in this tiny, white paint-peeling bar and watch a genius at work. Here in one of the poorest regions of Ohio. Here on a mountain, the summer spice fresh outside and the cheap draft beer as fresh as it got on the inside. Here, with people slowly nodding their heads or grinding their hips on every side of him. He was here. He was watching his favorite musician doing his thing on stage, completely alone. Just Doos, an acoustic guitar and a sliding steel.

Part of Alistair Doos' popularity, without a doubt, was the sheer mystery surrounding his life. There were two or three really great books about Doos, one written by a man named Jack Napier, Nathan's colleague back in New York, but all of them were spun from the stories of relatives and acquaintances. Doos had never allowed an interview in his life. At the time when Doos would have granted an interview, nobody was asking and now, he simply wouldn't talk to people. Nathan thought it probably wasn't so much a Salingeresque retreat from fame as it was a simple, Bartlebylike, "I prefer not to." Nathan also gleaned from his readings that it was impossible for Doos not to be very wary of the human race.

Black Rosita's Man

Doos was born into the most abject poverty in Mississippi in a shack close to the river in a place that didn't have a name. His father ran out on the family that included Doos, his mother, three brothers and five sisters. Mrs. Doos dragged the family north to Ohio where she'd heard people were a little friendlier to black folk. She had heard wrong. The Doos family lost two children to murder and three of the five sisters were raped before they turned eighteen. Mrs. Doos died young, presumably killed by stress, and the children went their separate ways. But Alistair stayed in Sawmill because of a woman ten years his elder. The woman's name was Rosita Johnson.

Rosita was able to make some cash as a laundress and her job was enough to support Doos in his drinking and music endeavors. According to the folks in the town, they had never seen two happier people. When Alistair wasn't playing his music, they were running around the town, drinking and making friends. And whenever Rosita could get the time off, she and Alistair traveled, Doos playing in whatever clubs would have him. There were rumors of a contract and then the bottom dropped out for blues. Alistair and Rosita looked around and found an America that was now heavy into jazz.

But this didn't discourage Alistair, he was still able to make some cash playing locally and Rosita put in some extra hours at the laundry. Then the bottom dropped out for Alistair and the lovely Rosita.

A crazed preacher from the town proper decided to turn Alistair and Rosita into a moral lesson. The preacher, William Kerch, said a lot of things about them that didn't make any sense like—"The colored folks shouldn't be given the power to run around this town acting the way they do." But the thing he said that people listened to was, "It's a sin for them two coloreds to be livin like they do." By that he meant unmarried. So the Reverend Kerch assembled a lynch mob and went up to the house of Alistair Doos and Rosita Johnson. He fired one shot into each of them as they slept and had his goons haul them out and string them up by their necks from a tree. As the mob stole back into the night, Kerch whispered into the small space between their dangling bodies, "I hope you both rot in hell."

The town was slightly perplexed but, in Sawmill, Ohio in the '40s, popular entertainment rated a great deal lower than old time religion. So they kept their mouths shut. The one thing the townsfolk decided on was that it was more likely Rosita Johnson was living in hell than Alistair Doos because, two weeks later, Doos walked into Hinkle's Grocery and bought the same things he'd bought since old Hinkle could remember: a fifth of whiskey, a carton of unfiltered Camels, a loaf of bread, a jar of peanut butter and a jar of apple butter. When he checked out he told old Hinkle, "Reverend said I should rot in hell. The way I figger, this here place's as close a man can get." Hinkle didn't take that to mean his grocery store.

For the next thirty years, Alistair would make the same trip and buy the same things. No one ever talked to him or went to his house because they were, quite simply, terrified as hell. The first year or so, he would occasionally enter the town sporting a garish white face and wearing a blond wig. On these occasions he'd say things to Hinkle like, "Just tryin to fit in." It was this white face that earned him the title, "The Ghoul from the Holler." Rumors had it Reverend Kerch had got so freaked out that he skipped the state of Ohio completely.

After that first year, Doos never said anything. Old man

Hinkle would say things to him and he would occasionally laugh, flashing a bone white smile, but he never said any words.

Then, in the early '90s he showed up at the Downtrod Inn, looking not much older than he had when the place was still called the Lookout. He played to a bar littered with five people. The reception was as grand as five people could give. Even though racial attitudes hadn't changed a whole lot, the old drunks could still appreciate virtuoso guitar picking. Doos came back every night, except for Sundays, and played. It was always the same. He carried his tattered black guitar case up to the stage and placed it by the scuffed brown chair. Then he walked over to the right of the stage and ascended the three steps. He sat down. He opened the case. He slid his belt buckle around to his hip, put the sliding steel over his left ring finger, picked up the guitar and let go. Sometimes he would play for fifteen minutes and sometimes he would play for three hours, never cracking a smile, never talking to anyone. When he was finished, he left by the exit behind the stage.

Slowly, the audience grew. They liked his stuff and some of the really old people thought his name sounded familiar but couldn't remember hearing anything by him. Eventually, a recording crew turned up. They showed Doos a contract. He signed it without reading it and began playing his set.

The only song he played consistently every night was "Black Rosita's Man." He seemed to add new verses all the time and Nathan must have heard about fifty versions of this song.

Nathan stood there, completely unaware he was sweating profusely, and listened to the magic coming from Doos' mouth and fingers. And visually, it came from his eyes.

Nathan felt like Doos must make eye contact with virtually every audience member—extended eye contact. It was like he played and sang almost absently while his eyes searched and probed. When Doos' near yellowish gaze fell on Nathan, he started wheezing. Nathan imagined that was what an asthma attack felt like. Clamps wrapped around his lungs. And that gaze was impossible to look away from. That gaze made Nathan think there was something about Alistair Doos no one really knew about.

What happened to Jack?

There was a depth, a dimension there, Nathan thought, most people only dream about.

And that's why they were all there. The locals were pale dirty ghosts scattered lazily around the back of the bar. The newcomers were early arrivals, filling the floor in front of the stage. Nathan knew something he thought none of them did. He knew where Doos lived.

Seeking out Doos' house had been the furthest thing from Nathan's mind when he had come down here. A naïve part of his intellect had told him he respected the old man's privacy too much for that. Something happened amidst the thumping of Doos' dusty shoe against the floor and the dry molasses moan of his voice and the steel chime of his thick fingernails picking the guitar. A feeling overwhelmed Nathan. It was a weird and beautiful feeling, filled with deep mystery. It was a feeling he hadn't felt since the summer when he was sixteen and the only black girl in the small town of Oracle, Kentucky, had introduced him to the magic of the moon and sex, the smell of clove cigarettes and the blues. She had taught him to love the blues and then taught him to feel the blues when she ran off with a musician from Cincinnati. But most of all, Nathan remembered the good feelings. The feeling a new world had opened up. Doos' gaze fell upon him and whined, "Follow me," and Nathan knew when Doos walked out that back door, he would be behind him.

That stare, that *feeling* was dangerous. He thought of other things, sliding steel liquid thoughts. Like where was Jack Napier? He had disappeared was all, Nathan told himself— *convinced* himself. Jack had come to Sawmill, intensely scrutinized a man living out life exactly the way he wanted to, nothing but solitude and music, and had decided to follow suit. Maybe Jack was holed up in some other small town, writing the Great American Novel he'd always talked about. The royalties from the Doos biography and the jazz textbook he'd sold a year earlier would certainly allow him to do that. It was Jack who had told Nathan where Doos lived but he didn't mention anything spectacular about it.

"The man goes inside. He comes out the next day to play," Jack had said. And yet this exercise in banality was something Nathan would have to observe for himself because he was here and he was alive and he was listening to that old man wail and he was looking into those eyes and he was so… *alive*, drunk off the moon and the smell of clove cigarettes and the blues the blues the blues.

Doos wound up his set, nodded his head in thanks, and folded up camp. There was no hope of getting past the crowd and following Doos out the back door. By the time Nathan squeezed past the lingering patrons and found his way out the front door, cutting quickly around the building, there was no trace of Doos.

You don't need to follow him, Nathan thought. *You know where it is.*

Nathan remembered that conversation, his last, with Jack very clearly.

"There's an opening in the woods behind the bar. Follow that and, after it starts to get really bushy, just try to stay as straight as you can. My guess is old Doos walks that path every night and then shoots off in some slight other direction so no particular path gets worn down. Keep going straight until you reach the clearing. It's a long way."

Then Jack had said: "I know I can trust you with this, Nathan." That was one of the only times he could remember Jack ever using his name in conversation.

Was there something panicked in that last conversation? Was there any hint Jack was going to disappear off the fucking planet?

Nathan's mind raced, emotions chasing themselves in circles.

He hasn't been gone that long, he told himself. And no, Nathan knew Jack and he hadn't sounded panicked in the least. He had sounded completely blissful. Nathan remembered, after getting off the phone with him, he had thought Jack sounded like someone who'd had a near death experience or found God or… or something else. Something that meant much more to a staunch atheist like Jack.

Cars were parked four rows deep behind the Downtrod Inn and Nathan wormed his way in between. The moon was a night away from being full and Nathan's vision was greatly helped by its purplish glow. He found the opening in the woods after only a minute's search. Once inside, he knew he would be away from the moon's nurturing glow. His vision reached no more than a couple of feet into the woods but he could sense its secret world. The insects with their secret language chirped and hummed, scurrying. He could smell the damp wood, resting up for another day of growth, however slight. And he could smell the sweet decay of the leaves, layered on the ground from a hundred sad and magical autumns.

He took a deep breath and began walking. He listened for the sound of the man in front of him but didn't hear so much as a broken twig or the soft swish of a leafy branch. No amount of paranoia could stop him, Nathan knew.

This world was far removed from his apartment in New York. There were no blaring horns or screeching trains or squealing cars or sirens and, perhaps most unsettling, there were no people. The woods were like nothing and everything, timeless.

More to keep himself company than anything else, Nathan began playing Alistair Doos' music in his head. The time flew by as quickly as it had at the bar.

Soon he reached the dead end.

"Keep walking straight," Jack had said.

Where are you, Jack? Nathan asked himself and the question was followed by that night's "Black Rosita's Man," still fresh in his head; there to comfort him, to ward away paranoia. *Follow me.* To guide him into something he hadn't felt in a long time.

The terrain rose uphill a little more, but Doos' music was there in his head, biology's iPod, to carry him on. Fallen sticks barked his shins, thin limbs scratched at his cheeks. That music, thick and sweet.

And there it was. Gleaming as white as the teeth in Doos' head, his house sat humbly in a large grassy circle.

Nathan stayed at the perimeter of the woods. The whole clearing seemed to glow, the moon reflecting off the house. The bargain iPod had turned itself off and Nathan tried to concentrate on what his next move would be.

Okay, you've seen it. You can go home now.

"The man goes inside. He comes out the next day to play."

There's nothing to see, right?

Except it seemed Doos hadn't just gone inside.

What happened to you out here, Jack?

Nathan heard the slow refrain of "Black Rosita's Man" coming from somewhere in that illuminated circle. It sounded almost too clear to be coming from within the house but Nathan couldn't see a trace of Doos.

He moved slowly to his right, crouching down into some of the smaller foliage. He continued moving cautiously and the music got closer. The night was almost chilly. Nathan found himself drawn to this sound, feeling brief flickers of warmth in his stomach. Nathan wanted to feel wrapped in it like he had back in the sweaty bar, like he had in the arms of the girl who'd graciously taken his virginity. He continued to move to his right.

Nathan found out why he had come.

The secret that lay behind Doos' slightly hooded eyes unfolded itself right there in front of him. It had all the elements of a completely fucked up dream but Nathan felt the warmth of the music and the chill of the night and he knew it was really happening.

Doos sat on a chair, plucking and singing away. He sang to a small tombstone at his feet. Nathan knew if he could read the tombstone it would say, "Rosita Johnson." The grass on top of the grave quivered. The air around Nathan was changing. It felt like the moments before a thunderstorm when the wind kicks up and the temperature is a schizophrenic swirl.

Doos played on.

Nathan couldn't tell if what he saw next was some sort of ghost or the real thing but there was Rosita Johnson, slowly taking form on top of her grave. She wasn't coming out of it the way zombies did in the movies. She was slowly becoming more… substantial, thicker, more *there*. And then, Nathan would have had to touch her to be a hundred percent certain, she *was* there.

She was Doos' music made flesh. All the beauty. All the pain. Nathan knew this was what Doos lived for. This was why he still played music. It wasn't for those adoring faces at the Downtrod Inn. It wasn't to be known as the best at anything. It was for love. For the love of Rosita Johnson.

He put down the guitar in the open case beside his chair.

What the fuck was Jack talking about? There's nothing to see! *What the hell* was *this?*

Doos laughed. A sweet sound, rich and loud.

"I missed you, old girl," he said.

It was Rosita's turn to laugh, shrill but filled with joy—"I missed *you*, old man," as though they had said this countless times before.

They embraced, turning in circles under the moonlight. Doos picked her up, cradling her in his arms.

Nathan turned to run. Not out of fear but out of guilt. He felt like he shouldn't have, no, he felt like it wasn't his *right*, to see what he had just seen. He tried running but his heartbeat slowed and thickened in his chest and his legs rubberbanded him to the ground.

He threw his head wildly up at the moon. The moon mocked him and he lowered his head to see a hundred other leering moons coming toward him from the dark mass of the forest.

Some of them were faces he recognized from the bar. And in the front, grinning wildly, was a face Nathan knew very well.

"Jack?"

"I found it, Nathan," Jack said. His blondish hair was longer than Nathan remembered, hanging almost down to his shoulder.

All those moons were coming closer.

"I swear I didn't tell anybody else, Jack." Why was he suddenly so afraid of Jack?

The eyes, Nathan thought. They contained a touch of Doos.

"Now you've found it, too," Jack said.

Jack put his hands on Nathan's sweaty face and turned it around, back toward the house. The rest of the people moved in tightly, forming a crescent around him.

Nathan's muscles, already stiff with fear, tightened even more.

Another moon face was quickly constructing a makeshift gallows from a tree beside Doos' house, behind the tombstone.

Doos and Rosita were dancing off to the gallows' right, singing a mock jazz duet.

"*We're gonna live for eternity,*" Doos sang.

"*Just you n me,*" Rosita sang.

"Bay-*beee*," they sang together.

Nathan shivered violently. He heard his teeth clacking in his head like some form of mad music behind the lovers' duet.

Jack pulled him up by one of his arms. The crescent moved in on him, lifting him up, carrying him toward the gallows.

"The mystery is darkening," Jack said.

"*I told you that sky was filled with holes,*" Rosita sang.

"*Don't waste yer breath on me, I'm out collectin souls,*" Doos half-sang, half-laughed.

The mob carried Nathan past the tombstone and he noticed it said, "Rosita Doos," not "Rosita Johnson."

Black Rosita's Man

"Why don't we get married, baby?" Doos.

"Just you n me..." Rosita.

The noose over the branch creaked.

"None of us should have done this, Nathan," Jack said.

"No," Nathan didn't know if he was protesting or agreeing. He screamed. He heard his scream rolling over those hills.

"Kerch will take care of you."

The Reverend Kerch placed the noose around Nathan's neck.

Doos laughed and began strumming, "Black Rosita's Man."

The crowd stepped away.

Nathan dropped.

He felt his neck snap and he felt the red shivers of pain bursting in his skull and he waited, but he didn't feel death. He felt fire. But it was just a feeling and he opened his eyes and everything he saw was hallucination red.

The hands tore away the clothes from his body.

The teeth bore down on him and he could hear the punctures more than feel them.

He looked down and Doos' mouth was clamped on his left wrist, Rosita's on his right.

"Let these two be joined!" the Reverend Kerch shouted. "Let these two be joined!"

The next night, Nathan looked at the fresh faces that had come to the Downtrod Inn. He was pressed back against the bar. He turned and looked toward Doos' eyes but those eyes didn't meet his. They looked at the sea below the stage, searching. Outside, the moon was full. The faint smell of cloves drifted in from outside, drowning out the sweat and the beer smells. And, in the slow coursing of his veins, Nathan felt the blues.

Rayles

They stacked the skulls on the south side of the tracks.

They didn't know what else to do with them.

Nissa grimaced with the weight of the skull-laden bag slung over her left shoulder. Sarot had an easier time dealing with his. Sarot was Nissa's younger brother. Younger but stronger. Dressed in dirty gray rags, Nissa sat her heavy canvas bag down and gestured for Sarot to do the same.

"Why are we holding up?!" he shouted. The train, Rayles, circled the town constantly and, here, so close to it, normal conversation was impossible. Everything was a shout.

"We should rest for a few minutes before going up! It's a long climb!" Nissa shouted back.

She looked across the town. The sad, depressing town, cloaked in perpetual gloom, the huge and angry black train circling it, surrounding it, the engine car always chasing the caboose, separated only by inches. Since the train never stopped, it made escape impossible.

Impossible, maybe, but tonight escape was exactly what Nissa and Sarot intended to do. These last two bags of skulls, these were their tools. They had practiced for this night. All they had to do was carry the skulls to the top of the mountain—the same ritual that had been performed for years—and then... Well, that was the mystery. They didn't know what came after that. No one did. Except maybe Rayles.

Sarot cleared his throat. He was an exceptionally serious and morose boy even for a town that turned out hardly anything except serious and morose boys. "Why hasn't anyone just built a ladder or something like that to get out?!" Still the shouting. It added a sort of jocularity to a very serious question.

Nissa looked guiltily at the ground. She should have told him the whole story. She should have told him the whole story a long time ago. Now, it was too late. And she would have to shout the whole thing anyway. The story was far too serious to even attempt conveyance by shouting.

"It wouldn't work!" she yelled.

"Why not?!"

"It just... wouldn't work, okay?!"

"Okay, but I don't understand why!"

"Sometimes it's best not to understand why!"

Indeed, that was the truest thing she had said to the boy since he was born. She didn't think he needed to understand why everything had dried up. Why there were hardly any people left in the town. Why they had been here for so long, since birth, held prisoner. Why the people in town didn't look the way they used to. Why they were now gray, some of them mutated so much they could be considered human only by the broadest of standards. It was solidarity, Nissa thought. Any human, no matter how monstrous, was better than that thing circling them, trapping them.

And no, she didn't really think he needed to know about Rayles. How the train was more an extension of the conductor than a piece of machinery.

He had once innocently asked her what kind of cargo the train carried and why it never seemed to go anywhere except in circles. She couldn't remember how she had skirted the question but she had.

"We should start up now," Nissa said loudly, tired of shouting.

"Huh?!" Sarot blared.

Nissa pointed up to the top of the mountain of skulls sweeping toward them from the train. "We should go now!"

"Oh! Okay!"

Nissa repositioned her bag of skulls, now shifting it back to the other shoulder, and led the way. It had not been their turn to climb the mountain for six months. Last time, it had taken just over an hour. Nissa wondered how many skulls had been added by the other townsfolk during those months.

They had to tread very carefully. One wrong step and the whole mountain of skulls could come tumbling down. Then the townsfolk would have to spend days rebuilding them. To do so could, quite possibly, attract the attention of Rayles himself. Although there had never been so much as a story about Rayles leaving the engine to come down to the town, she didn't want to think about the further horrors awaiting them if that actually happened.

She was amazed how the skulls had stayed this way, the pile growing larger and larger, over the years. Perhaps Rayles was merely toying with them. Maybe he was too busy tending to his other duties to care. Maybe he didn't think the townsfolk would be around long enough for the mountain to become a threat. Or maybe something even worse waited for them on the other side. That thought had crossed her mind quite a lot over the past few months, ever since learning she and Sarot would be the ones to attempt this feat.

Poor Sarot. If his life ended tonight, he would never know the story behind his death. But Nissa would. It was a story she knew all too well. It had been told to her in the cradle and she had heard it at least weekly until her mother had met her end trying to escape the snaking iron and steel that was Rayles.

Sarot had asked about ladders. He should have asked his father. His father who, as one of the strongest men in town, had been elected to hold the mammoth ladder while the women tried to climb it.

The women were the first to be consumed in the blaze. Rayles' cars growing orange-hot before the fire erupted from the windows, turning the wood ladder to cinder and teaching a valuable lesson to the townsfolk.

They were no longer here by choice.

Nissa remembered her father's weeping, his blackened arms and singed eyebrows. It wasn't long after that he died. And Nissa, only twelve, had become something of a mother to Sarot.

Rayles was born in a day when humans had godlike abilities. They erected cities and castles. They invented flight. They invented industry and commerce. And the only thing Rayles had wanted was a perfect little town. So he had made Uroboros. Gleaming silver and loaded with cargo, it circled three miles of lush land.

Sometimes Nissa wondered what the town had been like before the decay, when it still had a name. When people dreamt things and those dreams came true. Hadn't this town once been the dream of Rayles? She saw signs of that old life—the houses built along the perimeter of the town, along the tracks, because Rayles used to bring them something other than misery. And people had flocked to the once green valley where there was no want for anything. Food, shelter, warmth, beauty, leisure, a good sex life—it was all brought by the man who had built the gleaming silver train and promised people that, in his town, people's dreams would always have a home.

But Rayles got sick. Apparently, he was not godlike enough to avoid illness. Only he wouldn't die, he couldn't, because his dream was immortality. Immortality and the train he had made.

Deals with the devil were mentioned. The rumor was that Rayles would be able to live eternally if he agreed to carry the souls of the damned on his train. Hell, it seemed, was full.

Townspeople noted the changes in Rayles and in the train itself. Rayles grew gaunt. His eyes grew yellow. His hair grew long and gray, trailing out behind him. Not that anyone could get that close a look.

The train stopped stopping. Not only that, it seemed to go faster and faster. It made people dizzy just to look at it. It became black with soot because it never stopped to be washed.

And there were the faces.

That was the most shocking change of all.

The cargo.

These were not the goods and services Rayles once delivered.

Through the windows of the cars, the townspeople could see the faces of the damned, staring out from the grimed over windows, longing for anywhere other than the inside of that train. Sometimes there were screams. Screams of such volume that they rivaled the rumbling, jangling sound of the train itself. And the whistle changed too, sounding very much like a scream itself. Nearly every minute, it loosed one of its shrieks.

Nissa was conscious of all this as they neared the top of the skulls.

The engine car went past and she swore she heard Rayles laughing from inside.

Did he know? she wondered. Did he know what they had planned?

The skulls were those of friends and family, neighbors. Some of them had died trying to escape. Some of them had died trying to reclaim the world beyond Rayles' tyranny. For some, that world was a green memory. For others, it was a dream, something unseen by any eye other than the mind's.

Nissa liked the idea of using the skulls to escape. It would be like using Rayles' victims against him. His very evil would be his downfall and her loved ones and acquaintances could experience a small scrap of revenge.

At the top, she cautiously unslung her pack and said, "Careful now!" to Sarot. It was a little less deafening here at the top of the mountain of skulls.

She began placing the skulls so they were every-other-one with the previous layer.

"I'm scared!" Sarot said.

"You should be scared!" she said, not comforting him at all. There wouldn't be any sense in filling the boy with false hope. Not at this point.

After emptying her bag, she gestured for his. He placed it gently down on the skulls and opened it up. She took them out one by one, hoping it would give them the leverage they needed. She wanted to be able to see what lay on the other side of Rayles. Hopefully, the mountain would be high enough to clear the train when they tried to jump it. She knew it would be a long fall down the other side but she felt like maybe a twisted ankle was worth it. A broken leg and fractured skull would have been worth it. Together, the brother and sister had worked on their jumping skills and now, staring at the width of the train from this vantage point, she didn't think they would have a problem clearing it.

A giddy excitement pounded in her chest. She wanted to be done with it. She wanted to taste freedom and get out of all this deafening gloom. Every second of hesitation was another link on their chain. Only, as she stared out at the impregnable blackness, she wasn't so sure of herself. She didn't know if she wanted to make the jump not knowing what was out there.

No.

They had to.

This was what they came for.

But she wasn't going to risk Sarot. She couldn't do that. How could she be sure there was anything out there at all? It had been a long time since Rayles had closed his town against the rest of the world.

Turning toward Sarot, she grabbed his shoulders.

"Listen to me," she said loudly. "You need to stay here. If there's something better out there then I'll come back for you and the rest of the townsfolk. If I don't come back... *make sure no one else attempts to escape*. Do you understand?"

The engine sped past again. She figured she had only a couple of minutes until he was all the way across town. His whistle shrieked.

Sarot wiped tears from his eyes and shouted, "But I wanna come too!"

"You can't," she said. "But I have to go quickly. Remember, tell the townsfolk what I said. Learn to make this your home. A better home."

The boy nodded.

She hugged him, felt his bony chest press against her. She released him and went into her crouch. She took a deep breath and sprang out into the night, sailing over Rayles.

She hit the rocky ground on the other side, crying out in pain as her knee buckled and her hip shattered. She managed to pull herself up on one leg, wincing at the explosions of hurt and the sight in front of her.

The world.

The world beyond Rayles.

The stink of death raped her nostrils.

Smoke and fire.

The world gone bad.

The whole sick world sprawled out dead before her.

And there were... *things* out there. Dead things, snarling as they rooted through ashes, rose from the dust, smelled the fresh meat and came toward her.

Desperately, she looked back toward Rayles. The engine was charging around the last turn.

The whistle shrieked and she saw the look of hurt in the dead things' eyes. But it wasn't enough to stop them. The scent of fresh meat—fresh, *obtainable* meat—was too strong. They scrabbled toward her, closing in from around her.

Nissa saw Rayles, reaching his long frail arms from the engine, trying to grab her, trying to save her.

But he was too old and too tired and the dead things were so hungry.

Other Grindhouse Press Titles

#010 – *King of the Perverts*
by Steve Lowe

#009 – *Sunruined: Horror Stories*
by Andersen Prunty

#008 – *Bright Black Moon: Vampires in Devil Town Book Two*
by Wayne Hixon

#007 – *Hi I'm a Social Disease: Horror Stories*
by Andersen Prunty

#006 – *A Life On Fire*
by Chris Bowsman

#005 – *The Sorrow King*
by Andersen Prunty

#004 – *The Brothers Crunk*
by William Pauley III

#003 – *The Horribles*
by Nathaniel Lambert

#002 – *Vampires in Devil Town*
by Wayne Hixon

#001 – *House of Fallen Trees*
by Gina Ranalli

#000 – *Morning is Dead*
by Andersen Prunty